BRICK by BRICK

By Charles R. Smith Jr.

Illustrated by
Floyd Cooper

Amistad
An Imprint of HarperCollinsPublishers

Amistad is an imprint of HarperCollins Publishers.

Brick by Brick. Text copyright © 2013 by Charles R. Smith Jr. Illustrations copyright © 2013 by Floyd Cooper. All rights reserved. Manufactured in China. No part of this book may be used or reproduced in any manner whatsoever without written permission except in the case of brief quotations embodied in critical articles and reviews. For information address HarperCollins Children's Books, a division of HarperCollins Publishers, 10 East 53rd Street, New York, NY 10022. www.harpercollinschildrens.com Library of Congress Cataloging-in-Publication Data is available. ISBN 978-0-06-192082-0

Typography by Dana Fritts. 12 13 14 15 16 SCP 10 9 8 7 6 5 4 3 2 1 ❖ First Edition

Dedicated to all the slaves who helped
build this country from the ground up.
—C.R.S. Jr.

In memory of my great-grandparents
Ricie and Mattie Banks.
—F.C.

Under a hazy,
hot summer sun,
many hands work
together as one.

The president of a new country
needs a new home,
so many hands work
together as one.

Black hands,
white hands,
free hands,
slave hands.

Slave hands dig,
saw,
and break stone,
laying the foundation
for the president's home.

Rented as property,
slave hands labor
as diggers of stone,
sawyers,
and bricklayers.

Diggers swing axes
to break up stone,
laying the foundation
for the president's home.

Jerry
Jess
Charles
Len

Dick
Bill
Harry
Jim

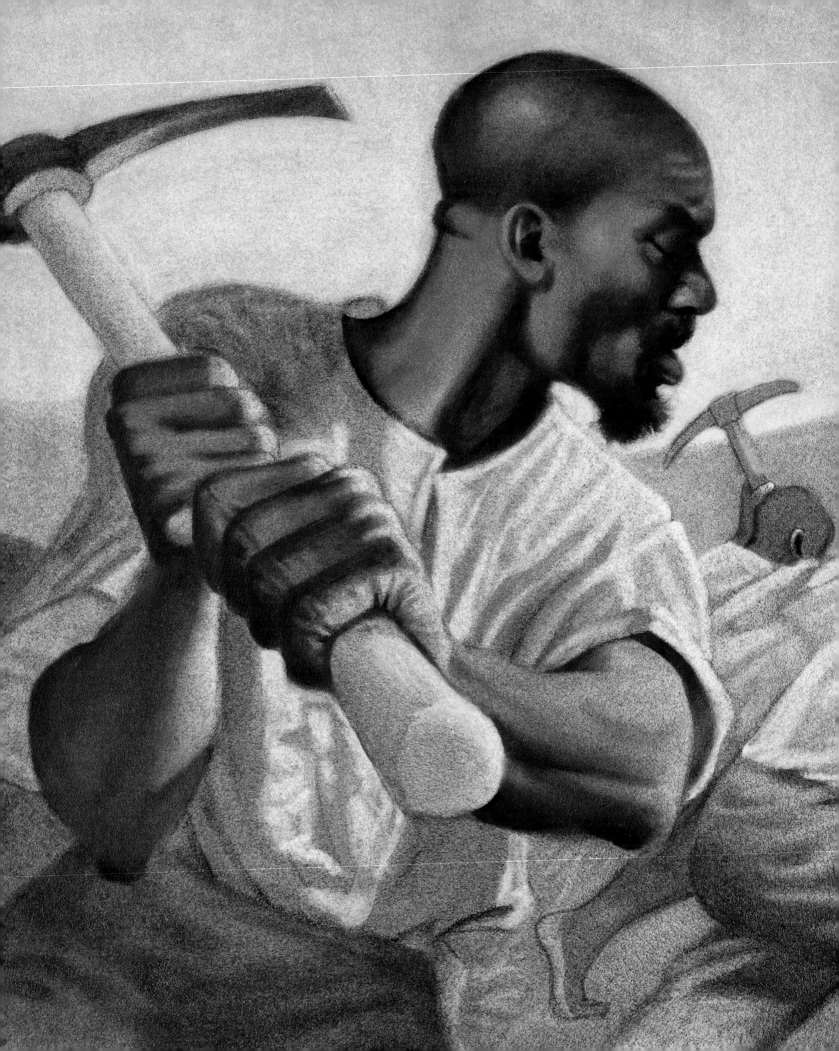

Slave hands swing axes
twelve hours a day,
but slave owners take
slave hands' pay.

Slave hands sweat
under a bright sun;
slave hands toil
until each day is done.

Chiseling, carving,
and transporting stone,
slave hands ache,
dark skin to white bone.

Slave hands blister
under a bright, hazy sun;
slave hands toil
until each day is done.

Sawyers saw blades
through logs of oak wood,
seven days a week
where a forest once stood.

Alick
Ben
William
Moses

Simon
Peter
Frank
Thomas

Up, down, push, pull,
two men per pit saw,
spraying sawdust
until slave hands are raw.

Slave hands saw
twelve hours a day,
but slave owners take
slave hands' pay.

Slave hands bleed
under a hot, hazy sun;
slave hands toil
until each day is done.

Clay, sand,
and water is mixed
by young slave hands
to create bricks.

Nameless, faceless
daughters and sons
build brick by brick
until each day is done.

Oystershells mixed
with rock, lime, and sand
become mortar for bricks
spread by slave hands.

Will
Nace
Gererd
Manuel

Liverpole
Lester
Herbert
Samuel

Slave hands spread mortar
twelve hours a day,
but slave owners take
slave hands' pay.

Slave hands crack
under a hot, hazy sun;
slave hands toil
until each day is done.

Slave hands learn
new trade skills
using chisels,
saws,
hammers,
and drills.

Skilled hands earn
one shilling per day,
reaching slave hands closer
to freedom with pay.

Brick by brick,
slave hands build;
day by day,
slave hands gain skill.

Month by month,
slave hands toil,
planting seeds of freedom
in fertile soil.

Freedom has a price
in a land of liberty,
so slave hands toil
to no longer be property.

Brick by brick,
where a forest once stood,
grows the president's home
made of stone and oak wood.

Slave hands build
and slave hands save
shillings to be free
and no longer a slave.

Slave hands count shillings
with worn fingertips
and purchase freedom
earned brick by brick.

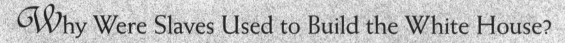

Why Were Slaves Used to Build the White House?

Today, we know that the White House exists in the big city of Washington, DC, but when construction began in 1792, it was in the middle of nowhere.

Manpower was needed to clear the forest, build the house, and make all the fine details inside. Lots of manpower. Local workers including immigrants from Scotland and other countries were hired, as well as free blacks, but it wasn't enough.

That's where slaves come in.

After realizing there weren't enough workers in the population to assist in construction, the government looked to slaves to round out the workforce. Slave owners from Virginia and Maryland received five dollars a month to rent out each slave. After a hard day of work, slaves returned to a small, shared hut and ate from the rations of pork, beef, and cornmeal provided to them.

Slaves endured a snake-infested island and mosquito swarms to dig up the stones needed for the walls of the house. They endured hour after hour of cutting and trimming wood, often until their hands were bloodied or deformed. The work was hard on the body, especially the hands.

I chose to focus on the hands because all of the work was done at a time when machines didn't exist to do those same jobs. "Hand" is also another name for a laborer or worker. Thus many slaves were needed to turn a wooded forest into our country's most famous address.

As the house began to be completed on the outside, skilled workers were needed to finish the inside. Skilled craftsmen from other countries taught the slaves trades such as cabinet making and carpentry. These skills allowed the slaves a chance to earn money and eventually pay for their freedom.

Unfortunately, the original White House was burned down by the British on the night of August 24, 1814, during the most dramatic episode of the War of 1812. It was later rebuilt and restored to its original condition, and stands as a reminder of the contribution made by slaves who worked toward freedom, brick by brick.

—Charles R. Smith Jr.

Selected Resources

Arnebeck, Bob. *Through a Fiery Trial: Building Washington 1790–1800*. Lanham, MD: Madison Books, 1991.

Holland, Jesse. *Black Men Built the Capitol: Discovering African-American History In and Around Washington, D.C.* Guilford, CT: Globe Pequot Press, 2007.

Office of the Architect of the Capitol: www.aoc.gov